Max Velthuijs
Frog in Love

Translated by Anthea Bell

A Sunburst Book / Farrar Straus Giroux

Frog was sitting on the riverbank.
He felt funny.
He didn't know if he was happy or sad.

He had been walking about in a dream all week.
What could be wrong with him?

Then he met Piglet.
"Hello, Frog," said Piglet. "You don't look very well.
What's the matter with you?"
"I don't know," said Frog. "I feel like laughing and crying at
the same time.
And there's something going thump-thump inside me, here."

"Maybe you've caught a cold," said Piglet.
"You'd better go home to bed."
Frog went on his way. He was worried.

Then he passed Hare's house.

"Hare," he said, "I don't feel well."

"Come along in and sit down," said Hare, kindly.

"Now then," said Hare, "what's the matter with you?"

"Sometimes I go hot, and sometimes I go cold," said Frog, "and there's something going thump-thump inside me, here."

And he put his hand on his chest.

Hare thought hard, just like a real doctor.

"I see," he said. "It's your heart. Mine goes thump-thump, too."

"But mine sometimes thumps faster than usual," said Frog.

"It goes one-two, one-two, one-two."

Hare took a big book down from his bookshelf and turned the pages.

"Aha!" he said. "Listen to this. Heartbeat, speeded up, hot and cold turns...It means you're in love!"

"In love?" said Frog, surprised. "Wow! I'm in love!"

And he was so pleased that he did a tremendous jump

right out of the door and up in the air.

Piglet was quite scared when Frog suddenly came falling from the sky.
"You seem to be better," said Piglet.
"I am! I feel just fine," said Frog. "I'm in love!"
"Well, that's good news. Who are you in love with?" asked Piglet.
Frog hadn't stopped to think about that.

"I know!" he said. "I'm in love with the pretty, nice, lovely white duck!"
"You can't be," said Piglet. "A frog can't be in love with a duck.
You're green and she's white."
But Frog didn't let that bother him.

He couldn't write, but he could do beautiful paintings.
Back at home he painted a lovely picture, with red and blue in it
and lots of green, his favorite color.

In the evening, when it was dark, he went out with his picture and pushed it under the door of Duck's house.
His heart was beating hard with excitement.

Duck was very surprised when she found the picture.
"Who can have sent me this beautiful picture?" she cried,
and she hung it on the wall.

Next day Frog picked a beautiful bunch of flowers.
He was going to give them to Duck.
But when he reached her door, he felt too shy to face her.
He put the flowers down on the doorstep and ran away as
fast as he could go.
And so it went on, day after day.
Frog just couldn't pluck up the courage to speak.

Duck was very pleased with all her lovely presents.
But who could be sending them?

Poor Frog!
He didn't enjoy his food anymore, and he couldn't sleep at night.
Things went on like this for weeks.

How could he show Duck he loved her?
"I must do something nobody else can do," he decided.
"I must break the world high jump record! Dear Duck will be very surprised, and then she'll love me back."

Frog started training at once.
He practiced the high jump for days on end.
He jumped higher and higher, right up to the clouds.
No frog in the world had ever jumped so high before.

"What can be the matter with Frog?" asked Duck, worried.
"Jumping like that is dangerous. He'll do himself an injury."
She was right.

At thirteen minutes past two on Friday afternoon, things went wrong.
Frog was doing the highest jump in history when he lost his balance and
fell to the ground.
Duck, who happened to be passing at the time,
came hurrying up to help him.

Frog could hardly walk. Supporting him carefully, she took him home
with her. She nursed him with tender loving care.
"Oh, Frog, you might have been killed!" she said. "You really must be
careful. I'm so fond of you!"
And then, at last, Frog plucked up his courage.
"I'm very fond of you too, dear Duck," he stammered. His heart was
going thump-thump faster than ever, and his face turned deep green.

Ever since then, they have loved each other dearly.
A frog and a duck...
Green and white.
Love knows no boundaries.